Hippo AND Rabbit

3 MORE TALES

BRAVE LIKE ME

Jeff Mack

Cartwheel
B·O·O·K·S®

SCHOLASTIC INC.

New York   Toronto   London   Auckland
Sydney   Mexico City   New Delhi   Hong Kong

—Table of— CONTENTS

For David Milgrim. That's M-I-L-G-R-I-M.

Copyright © 2011 by Jeff Mack.

All rights reserved. Published by Scholastic Inc.
SCHOLASTIC, CARTWHEEL BOOKS, and associated logos
are trademarks and/or registered trademarks of Scholastic Inc.
Lexile is a registered trademark of MetaMetrics, Inc.

No part of this publication may be reproduced, stored in a retrieval system, or transmitted in any form or by any means, electronic, mechanical, photocopying, recording, or otherwise, without written permission of the publisher. For information regarding permission, write to Scholastic Inc., Attention: Permissions Department, 557 Broadway, New York, NY 10012.

Hand-lettering & design by Angela Navarra
Text hand-lettering by Jeff Mack

ISBN 978-0-545-28360-1

16 15   19/0

Printed in the U.S.A. 40
First printing, November 2011

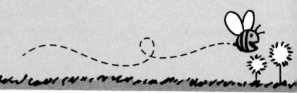

4

5

7

BALLOONS

Hey, Rabbit, I have a treat for us.

Oh boy! What is it?

24